OCT -- 2017

DATE DUE			

WITHDRAWN

Strawberry Shortcake™

Volume 3:
The Stuff Dreams Are Made Of

Written by: Georgia Ball
Art by: Amy Mebberson
Colors by: Fernando Peniche
Letters by: Tom B. Long

ABDO Spotlight   IDW

ABDOPUBLISHING.COM

Reinforced library bound edition published in 2018 by Spotlight, a division of ABDO
PO Box 398166, Minneapolis, Minnesota 55439. Spotlight produces high-quality
reinforced library bound editions for schools and libraries.
Published by agreement with IDW.

Printed in the United States of America, North Mankato, Minnesota.
042017
092017

THIS BOOK CONTAINS
RECYCLED MATERIALS

PUBLISHER'S CATALOGING IN PUBLICATION DATA

Names: Ball, Georgia ; Gudsnuk, Kristen, authors. | Mebberson, Amy ; Pena, Nico, illustrators.
Title: The stuff dreams are made of / writers: Georgia Ball ; Kristen Gudsnuk ; art: Amy Mebberson
; Nico Pena.
Description: Reinforced library bound edition. | Minneapolis, Minnesota : Spotlight, 2018. | Series:
Strawberry shortcake
Summary: A smooth-talking businessman tries to convince Strawberry Shortcake to expand her
bakery and she tries to sort out her decision in dreamland in the middle of a tense mystery. |
Bonus story summary (Yes to the Dress) Raspberry Torte and Strawberry Shortcake agree to
make very different dresses for Sweet and Sour Grapes, but the final reveal upsets Sour Grapes.
Identifiers: LCCN 2016961951 | ISBN 9781532140310 (vol. 3, lib. bdg.)
Subjects: LCSH: Strawberry Shortcake (Fictitious character)--Juvenile fiction. | Friendship--Juvenile
fiction. | Comic book, strips, etc.--Juvenile fiction. | Graphic novels--Juvenile fiction.
Classification: DDC 741.5--dc23
LC record available at https://lccn.loc.gov/2016961951

Spotlight

A Division of ABDO
abdopublishing.com

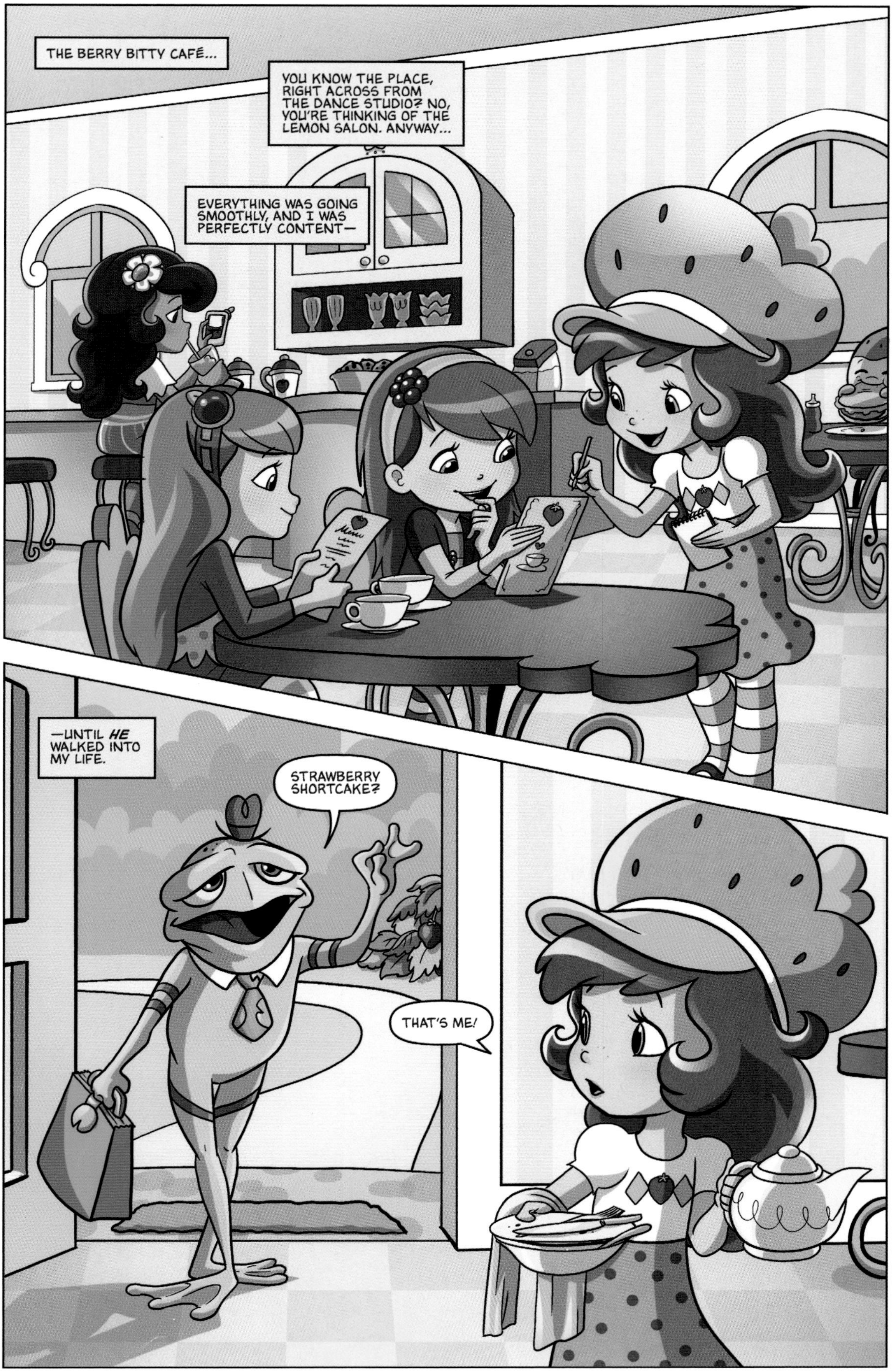
THE BERRY BITTY CAFÉ...
YOU KNOW THE PLACE, RIGHT ACROSS FROM THE DANCE STUDIO? NO, YOU'RE THINKING OF THE LEMON SALON. ANYWAY...
EVERYTHING WAS GOING SMOOTHLY, AND I WAS PERFECTLY CONTENT—
—UNTIL *HE* WALKED INTO MY LIFE.
STRAWBERRY SHORTCAKE?
THAT'S ME!

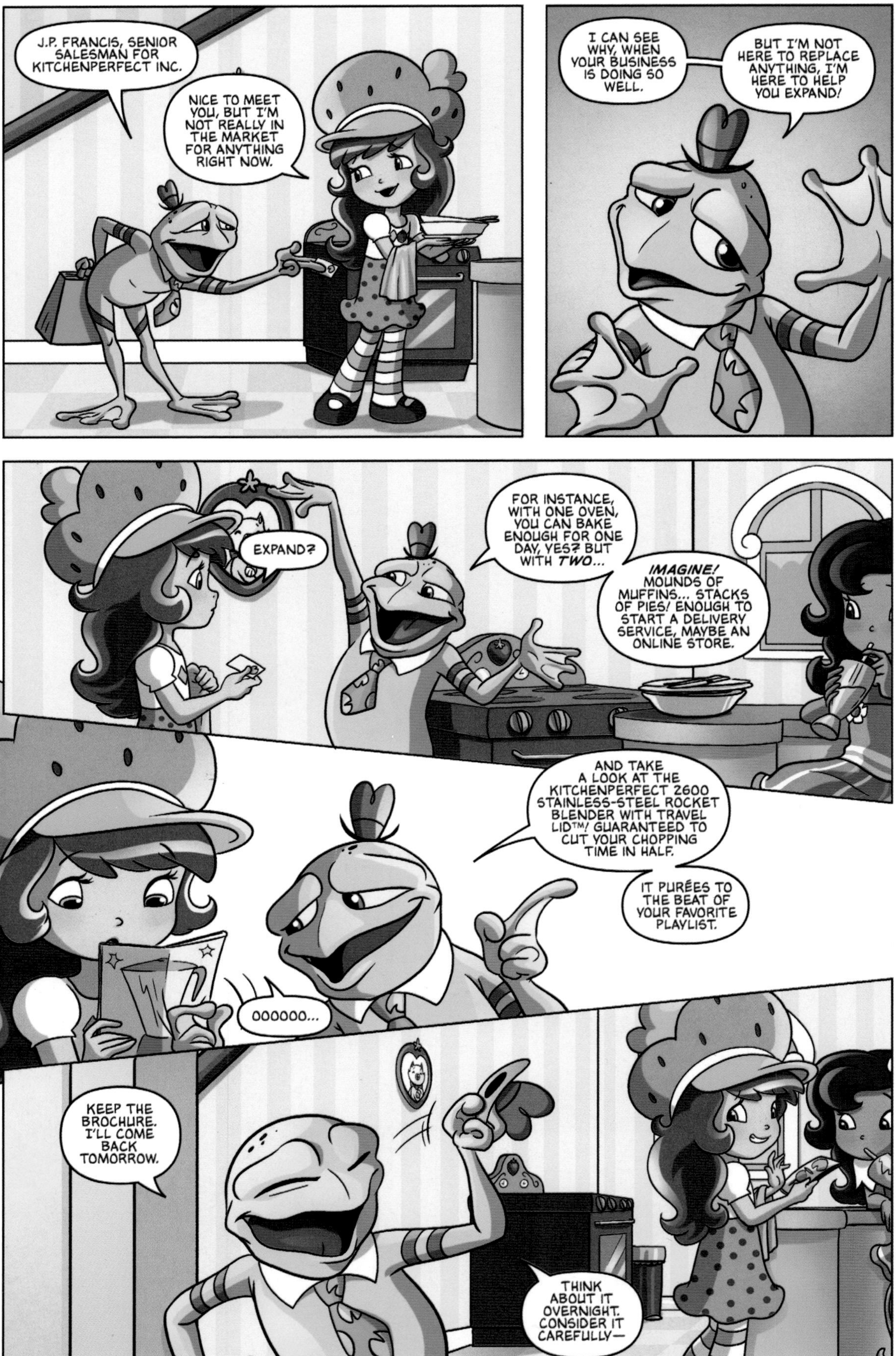
J.P. FRANCIS, SENIOR SALESMAN FOR KITCHENPERFECT INC.
NICE TO MEET YOU, BUT I'M NOT REALLY IN THE MARKET FOR ANYTHING RIGHT NOW.
I CAN SEE WHY, WHEN YOUR BUSINESS IS DOING SO WELL.
BUT I'M NOT HERE TO REPLACE ANYTHING, I'M HERE TO HELP YOU EXPAND!
EXPAND?
FOR INSTANCE, WITH ONE OVEN, YOU CAN BAKE ENOUGH FOR ONE DAY, YES? BUT WITH *TWO*...
IMAGINE! MOUNDS OF MUFFINS... STACKS OF PIES! ENOUGH TO START A DELIVERY SERVICE, MAYBE AN ONLINE STORE.
AND TAKE A LOOK AT THE KITCHENPERFECT 2600 STAINLESS-STEEL ROCKET BLENDER WITH TRAVEL LID™! GUARANTEED TO CUT YOUR CHOPPING TIME IN HALF.
IT PURÉES TO THE BEAT OF YOUR FAVORITE PLAYLIST.
OOOOOO...
KEEP THE BROCHURE. I'LL COME BACK TOMORROW.
THINK ABOUT IT OVERNIGHT. CONSIDER IT CAREFULLY—

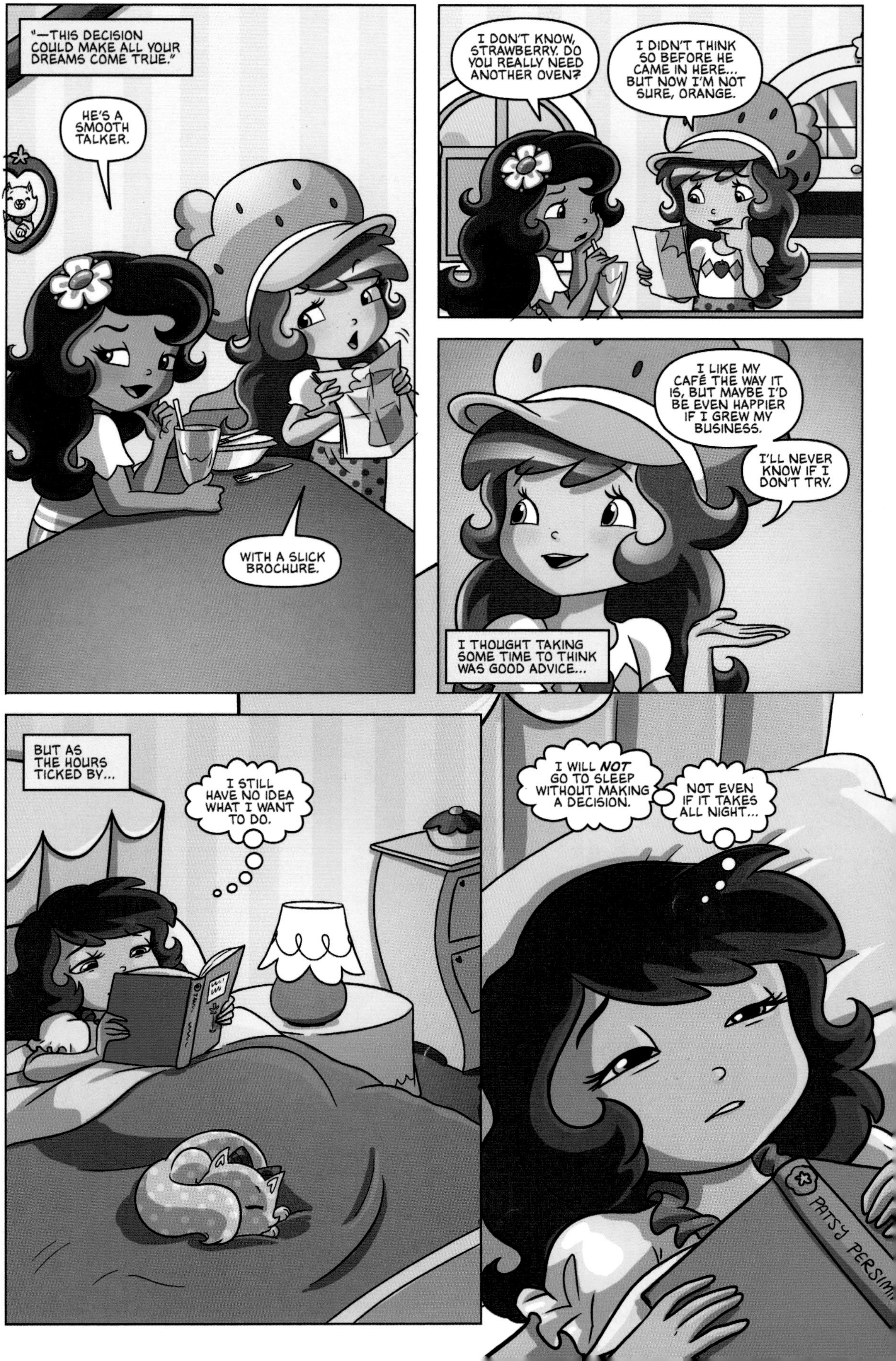
"—THIS DECISION COULD MAKE ALL YOUR DREAMS COME TRUE."
HE'S A SMOOTH TALKER.
WITH A SLICK BROCHURE.
I DON'T KNOW, STRAWBERRY. DO YOU REALLY NEED ANOTHER OVEN?
I DIDN'T THINK SO BEFORE HE CAME IN HERE... BUT NOW I'M NOT SURE, ORANGE.
I LIKE MY CAFÉ THE WAY IT IS, BUT MAYBE I'D BE EVEN HAPPIER IF I GREW MY BUSINESS.
I'LL NEVER KNOW IF I DON'T TRY.
I THOUGHT TAKING SOME TIME TO THINK WAS GOOD ADVICE...
BUT AS THE HOURS TICKED BY...
I STILL HAVE NO IDEA WHAT I WANT TO DO.
I WILL *NOT* GO TO SLEEP WITHOUT MAKING A DECISION.
NOT EVEN IF IT TAKES ALL NIGHT...
PATSY PERSIM

I NEEDED TO GIVE THIS PROBLEM MY FULL ATTENTION...

ZZZZZZZZZZZZZZZZZZZZZZZZZZ

WAKE UP, STRAWBERRY... WE HAVE A CLIENT!

SNERK

WE HAVE A WHAT-NOW?

SOMEONE HAS A CASE FOR OUR STRUGGLING DETECTIVE AGENCY?

DON'T TELL ME IT'S BEEN SO LONG YOU'VE FORGOTTEN WHAT A CLIENT LOOKS LIKE.

CASE CLOSED

I'LL GO GET HER.

A QUICK GLANCE AROUND THE OFFICE CLUED ME IN...

I'M A DETECTIVE...

LOOK AT ALL THE MYSTERIES I'VE SOLVED! LIKE THE TIME WE HELPED... THAT BEE! AND THAT TIME WE— FOUND A NEEDLE IN A HAYSTACK?

WHY WOULD ANYONE WANT TO FIND A *LITERAL* NEEDLE IN A HAYSTACK? COULDN'T THEY JUST GET A NEW ONE?

WE CAN REMINISCE LATER...

THIS IS LADY BERRY.

CASE CLOSED

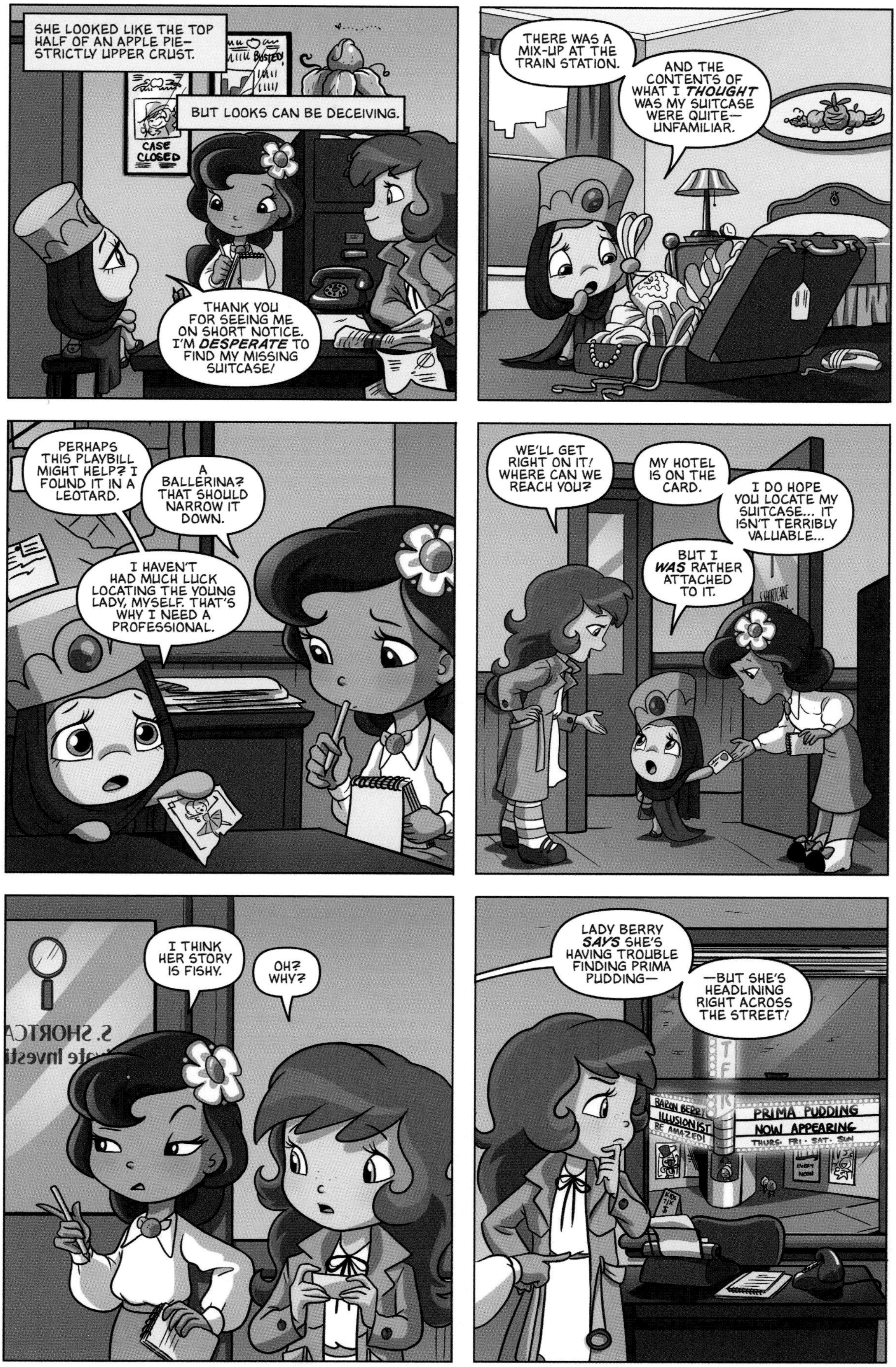

SHE LOOKED LIKE THE TOP HALF OF AN APPLE PIE— STRICTLY UPPER CRUST.
BUSTED!
CASE CLOSED
BUT LOOKS CAN BE DECEIVING.
THANK YOU FOR SEEING ME ON SHORT NOTICE. I'M DESPERATE TO FIND MY MISSING SUITCASE!
THERE WAS A MIX-UP AT THE TRAIN STATION.
AND THE CONTENTS OF WHAT I THOUGHT WAS MY SUITCASE WERE QUITE— UNFAMILIAR.
PERHAPS THIS PLAYBILL MIGHT HELP? I FOUND IT IN A LEOTARD.
A BALLERINA? THAT SHOULD NARROW IT DOWN.
I HAVEN'T HAD MUCH LUCK LOCATING THE YOUNG LADY, MYSELF. THAT'S WHY I NEED A PROFESSIONAL.
WE'LL GET RIGHT ON IT! WHERE CAN WE REACH YOU?
MY HOTEL IS ON THE CARD.
I DO HOPE YOU LOCATE MY SUITCASE... IT ISN'T TERRIBLY VALUABLE...
BUT I WAS RATHER ATTACHED TO IT.
I THINK HER STORY IS FISHY.
OH? WHY?
LADY BERRY SAYS SHE'S HAVING TROUBLE FINDING PRIMA PUDDING—
—BUT SHE'S HEADLINING RIGHT ACROSS THE STREET!
BARON BERRY ILLUSIONIST BE AMAZED!
PRIMA PUDDING
NOW APPEARING
THURS · FRI · SAT · SUN

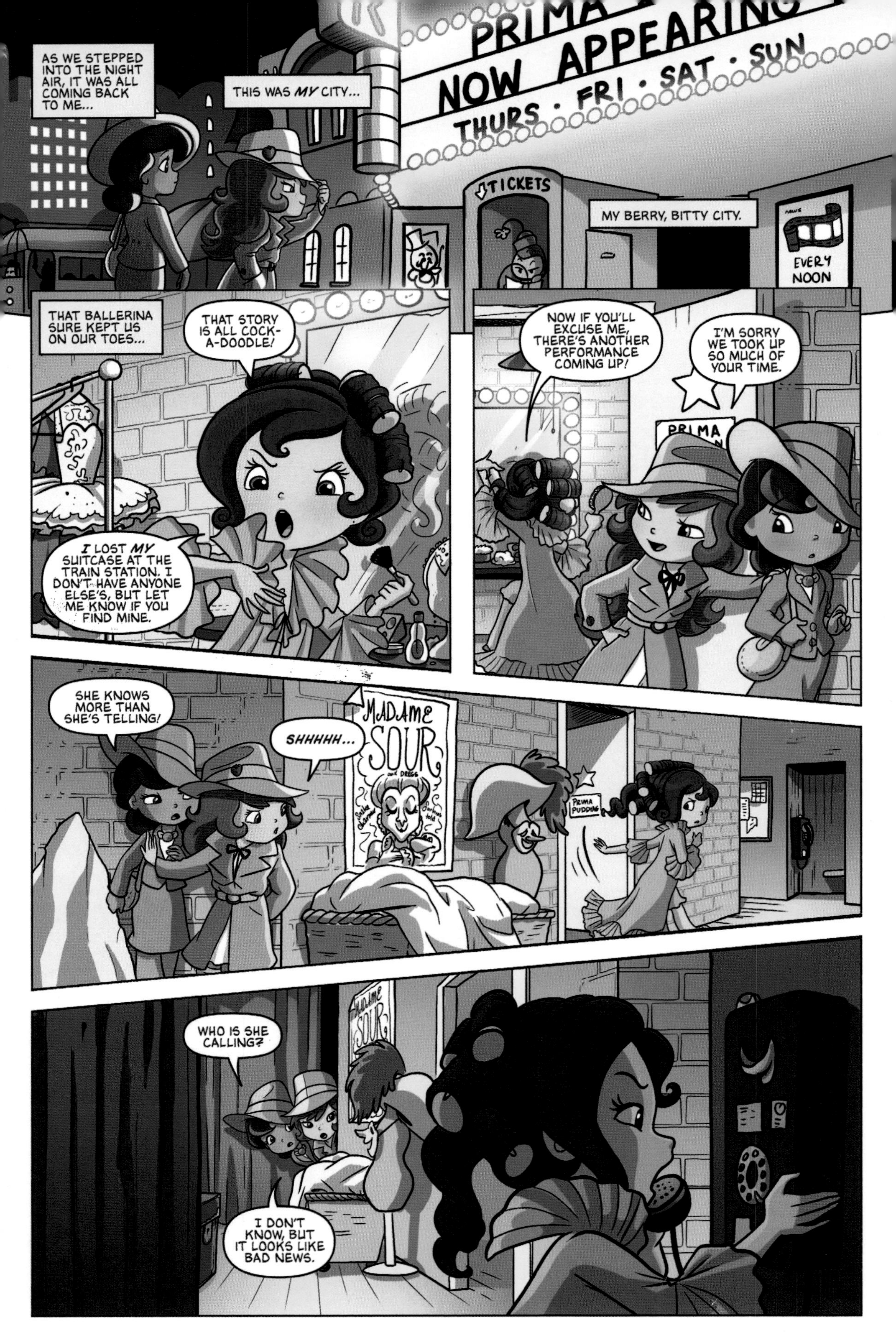
PRIMA
NOW APPEARING
THURS · FRI · SAT · SUN
AS WE STEPPED INTO THE NIGHT AIR, IT WAS ALL COMING BACK TO ME...
THIS WAS MY CITY...
TICKETS
MY BERRY, BITTY CITY.
EVERY NOON
THAT BALLERINA SURE KEPT US ON OUR TOES...
THAT STORY IS ALL COCK-A-DOODLE!
I LOST MY SUITCASE AT THE TRAIN STATION. I DON'T HAVE ANYONE ELSE'S, BUT LET ME KNOW IF YOU FIND MINE.
NOW IF YOU'LL EXCUSE ME, THERE'S ANOTHER PERFORMANCE COMING UP!
I'M SORRY WE TOOK UP SO MUCH OF YOUR TIME.
PRIMA
SHE KNOWS MORE THAN SHE'S TELLING!
SHHHHH...
MADAME SOUR
PRIMA PUDDING
WHO IS SHE CALLING?
MADAME SOUR
I DON'T KNOW, BUT IT LOOKS LIKE BAD NEWS.

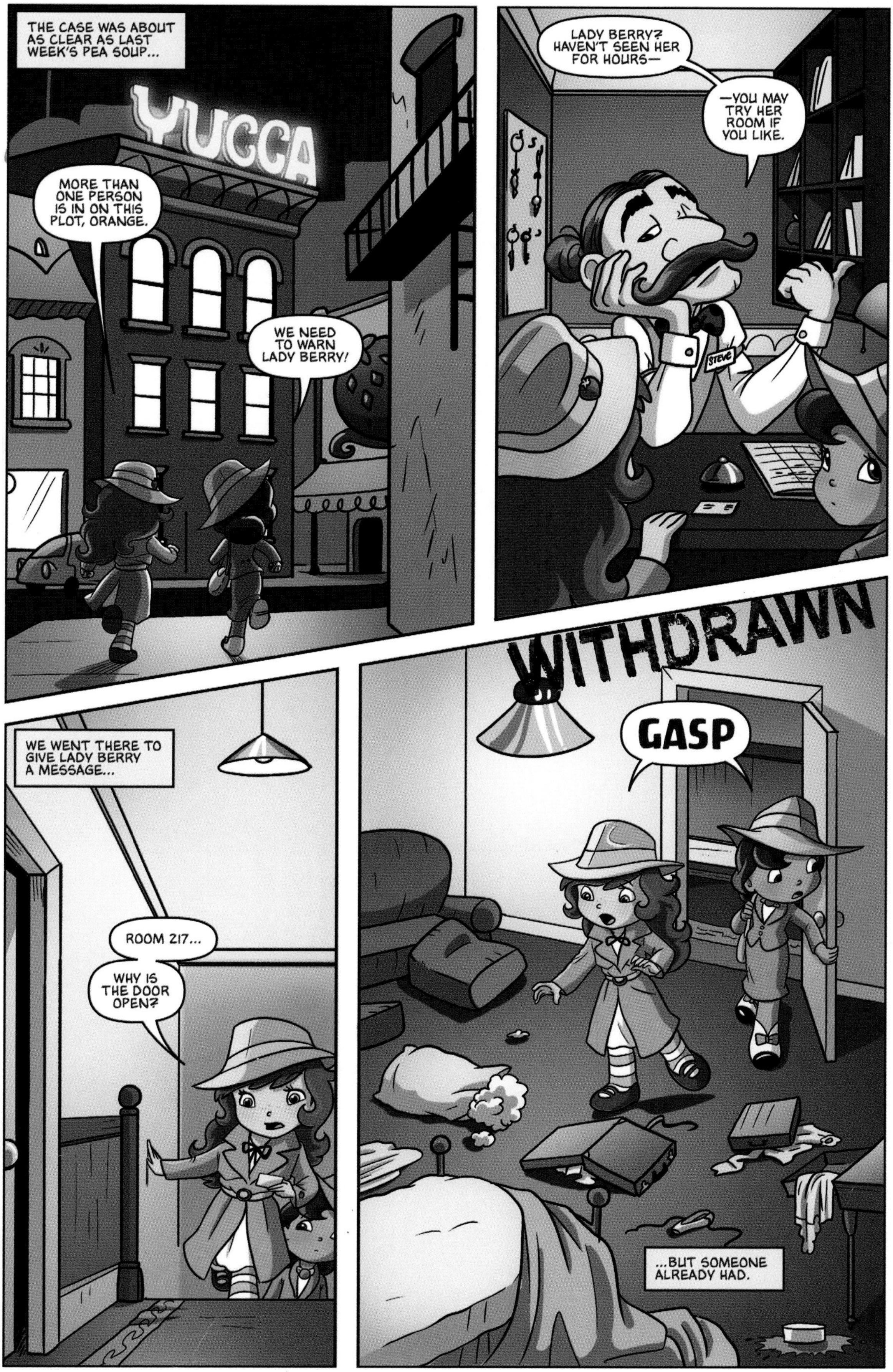
THE CASE WAS ABOUT AS CLEAR AS LAST WEEK'S PEA SOUP...
YUCCA
MORE THAN ONE PERSON IS IN ON THIS PLOT, ORANGE.
WE NEED TO WARN LADY BERRY!
LADY BERRY? HAVEN'T SEEN HER FOR HOURS—
—YOU MAY TRY HER ROOM IF YOU LIKE.
STEVE
WE WENT THERE TO GIVE LADY BERRY A MESSAGE...
ROOM 217...
WHY IS THE DOOR OPEN?
GASP
...BUT SOMEONE ALREADY HAD.

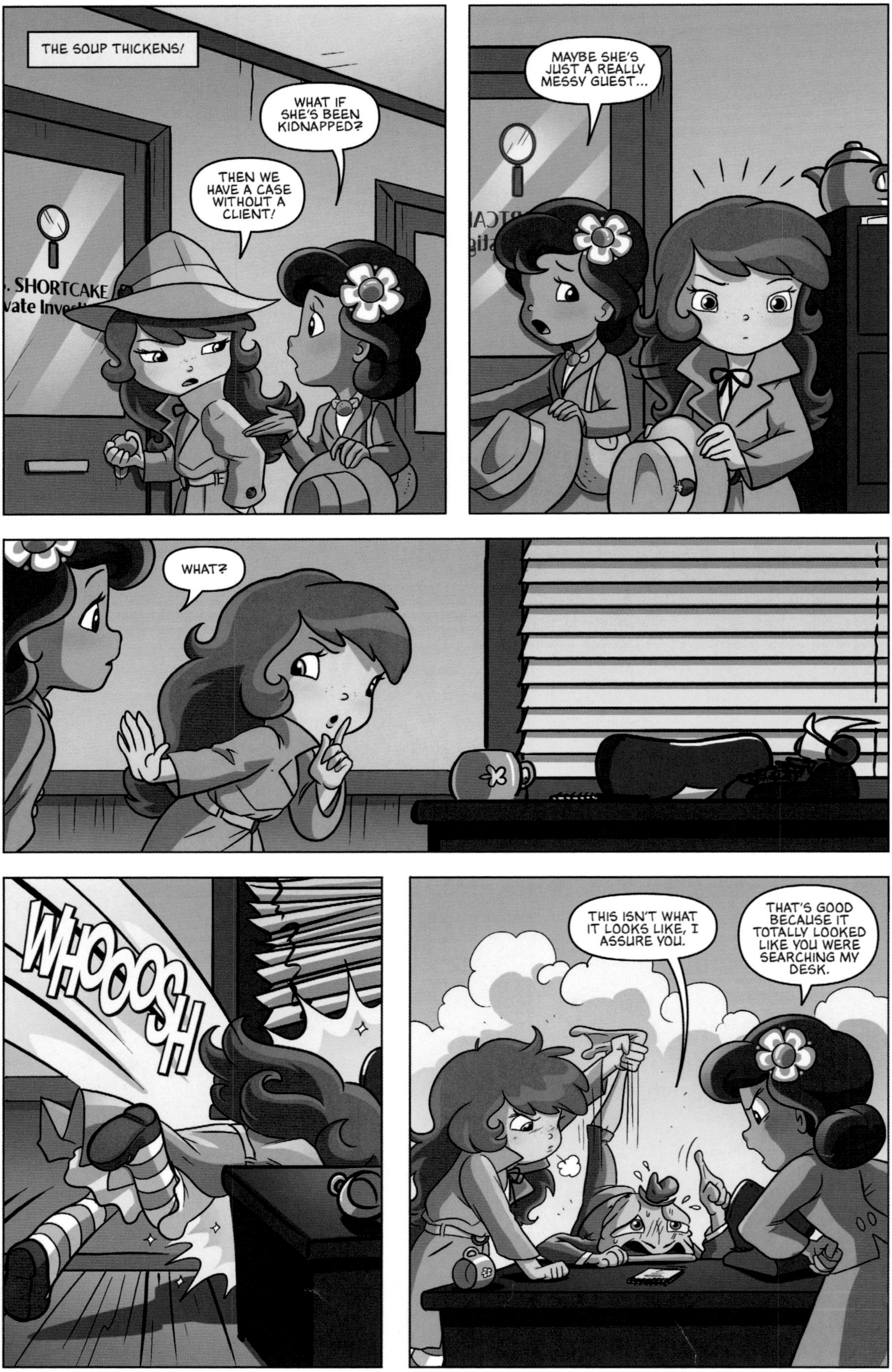
THE SOUP THICKENS!
WHAT IF SHE'S BEEN KIDNAPPED?
THEN WE HAVE A CASE WITHOUT A CLIENT!
. SHORTCAKE
vate Invest
MAYBE SHE'S JUST A REALLY MESSY GUEST...
WHAT?
WHOOOSH
THIS ISN'T WHAT IT LOOKS LIKE, I ASSURE YOU.
THAT'S GOOD BECAUSE IT TOTALLY LOOKED LIKE YOU WERE SEARCHING MY DESK.

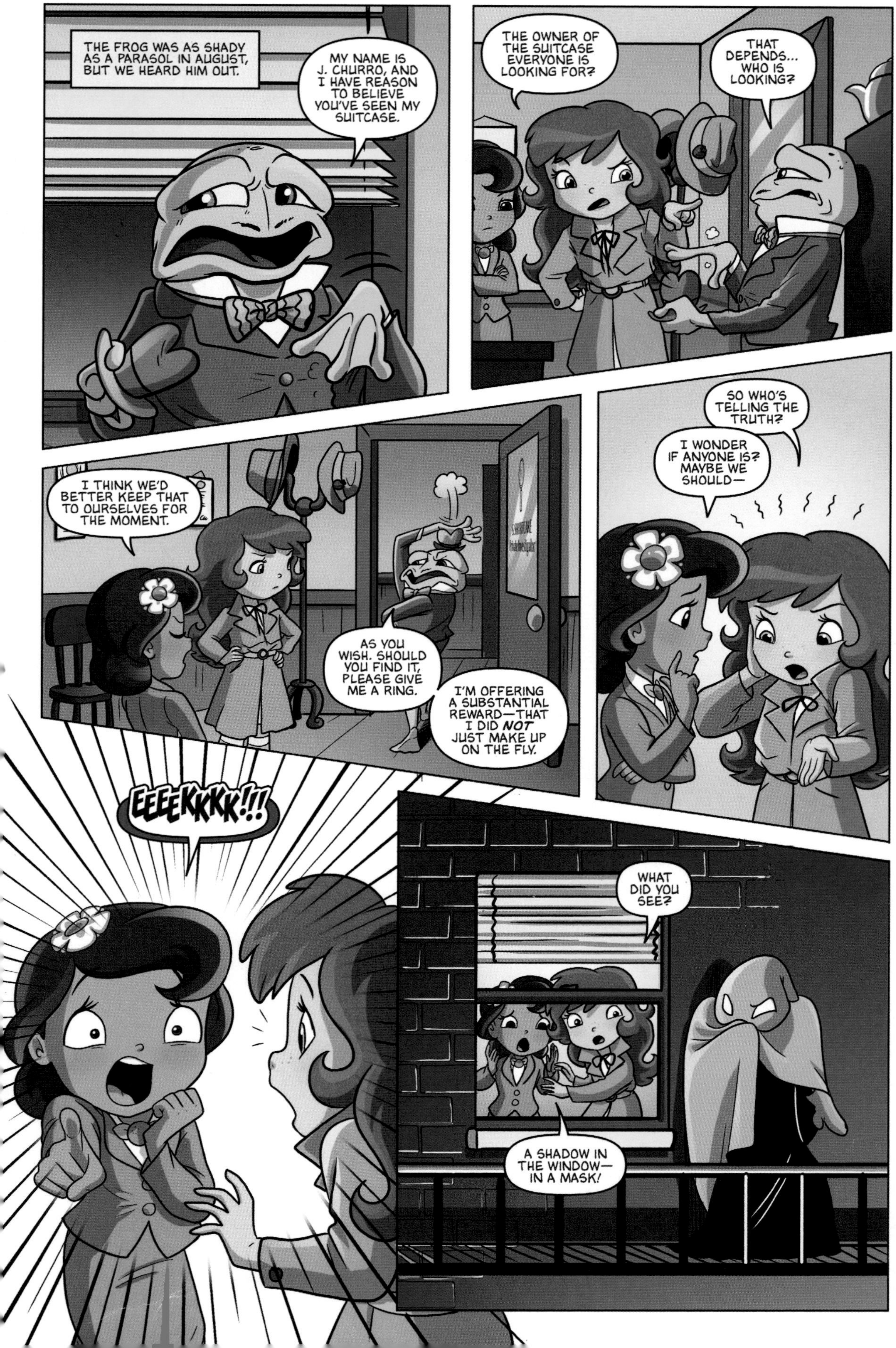
THE FROG WAS AS SHADY AS A PARASOL IN AUGUST, BUT WE HEARD HIM OUT.
MY NAME IS J. CHURRO, AND I HAVE REASON TO BELIEVE YOU'VE SEEN MY SUITCASE.
THE OWNER OF THE SUITCASE EVERYONE IS LOOKING FOR?
THAT DEPENDS... WHO IS LOOKING?
I THINK WE'D BETTER KEEP THAT TO OURSELVES FOR THE MOMENT.
AS YOU WISH. SHOULD YOU FIND IT, PLEASE GIVE ME A RING.
I'M OFFERING A SUBSTANTIAL REWARD—THAT I DID *NOT* JUST MAKE UP ON THE FLY.
SO WHO'S TELLING THE TRUTH?
I WONDER IF ANYONE IS? MAYBE WE SHOULD—
EEEEKKKK!!!
WHAT DID YOU SEE?
A SHADOW IN THE WINDOW—IN A MASK!

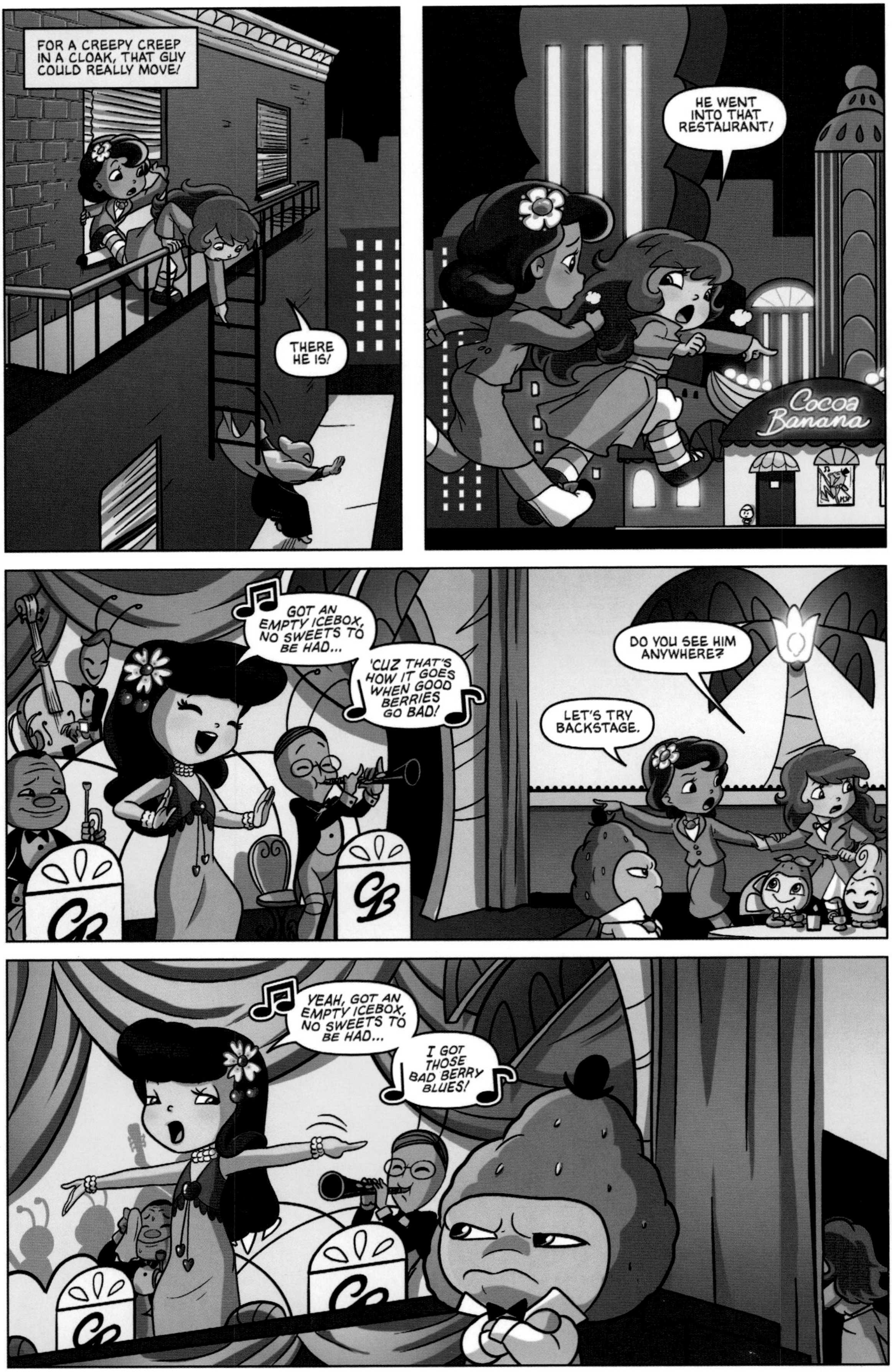
FOR A CREEPY CREEP IN A CLOAK, THAT GUY COULD REALLY MOVE!
THERE HE IS!
HE WENT INTO THAT RESTAURANT!
Cocoa Banana
GOT AN EMPTY ICEBOX, NO SWEETS TO BE HAD...
'CUZ THAT'S HOW IT GOES WHEN GOOD BERRIES GO BAD!
DO YOU SEE HIM ANYWHERE?
LET'S TRY BACKSTAGE.
YEAH, GOT AN EMPTY ICEBOX, NO SWEETS TO BE HAD...
I GOT THOSE BAD BERRY BLUES!

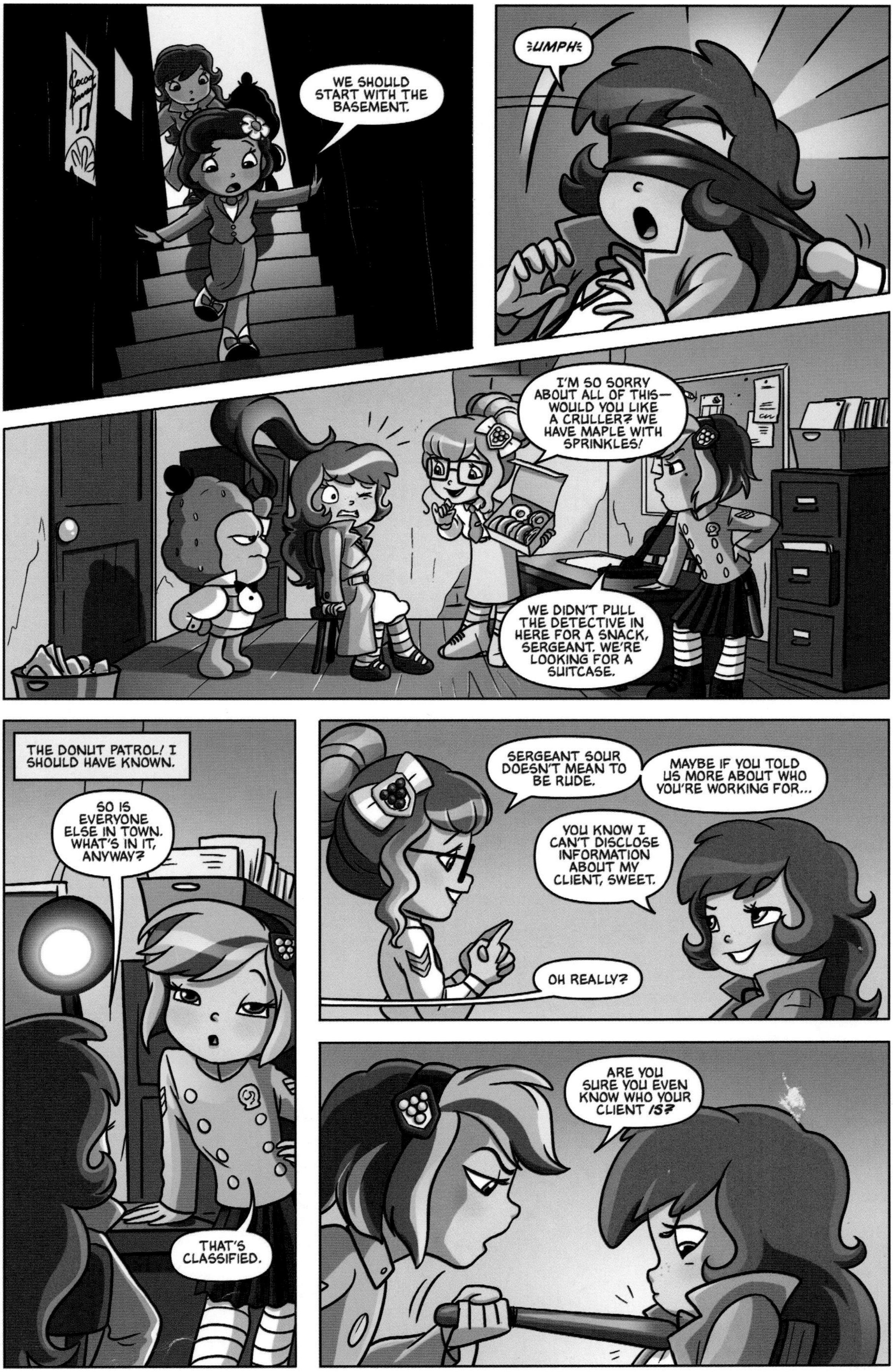
WE SHOULD START WITH THE BASEMENT.
UMPH
I'M SO SORRY ABOUT ALL OF THIS— WOULD YOU LIKE A CRULLER? WE HAVE MAPLE WITH SPRINKLES!
WE DIDN'T PULL THE DETECTIVE IN HERE FOR A SNACK, SERGEANT. WE'RE LOOKING FOR A SUITCASE.
THE DONUT PATROL! I SHOULD HAVE KNOWN.
SO IS EVERYONE ELSE IN TOWN. WHAT'S IN IT, ANYWAY?
THAT'S CLASSIFIED.
SERGEANT SOUR DOESN'T MEAN TO BE RUDE.
MAYBE IF YOU TOLD US MORE ABOUT WHO YOU'RE WORKING FOR...
YOU KNOW I CAN'T DISCLOSE INFORMATION ABOUT MY CLIENT, SWEET.
OH REALLY?
ARE YOU SURE YOU EVEN KNOW WHO YOUR CLIENT *IS*?

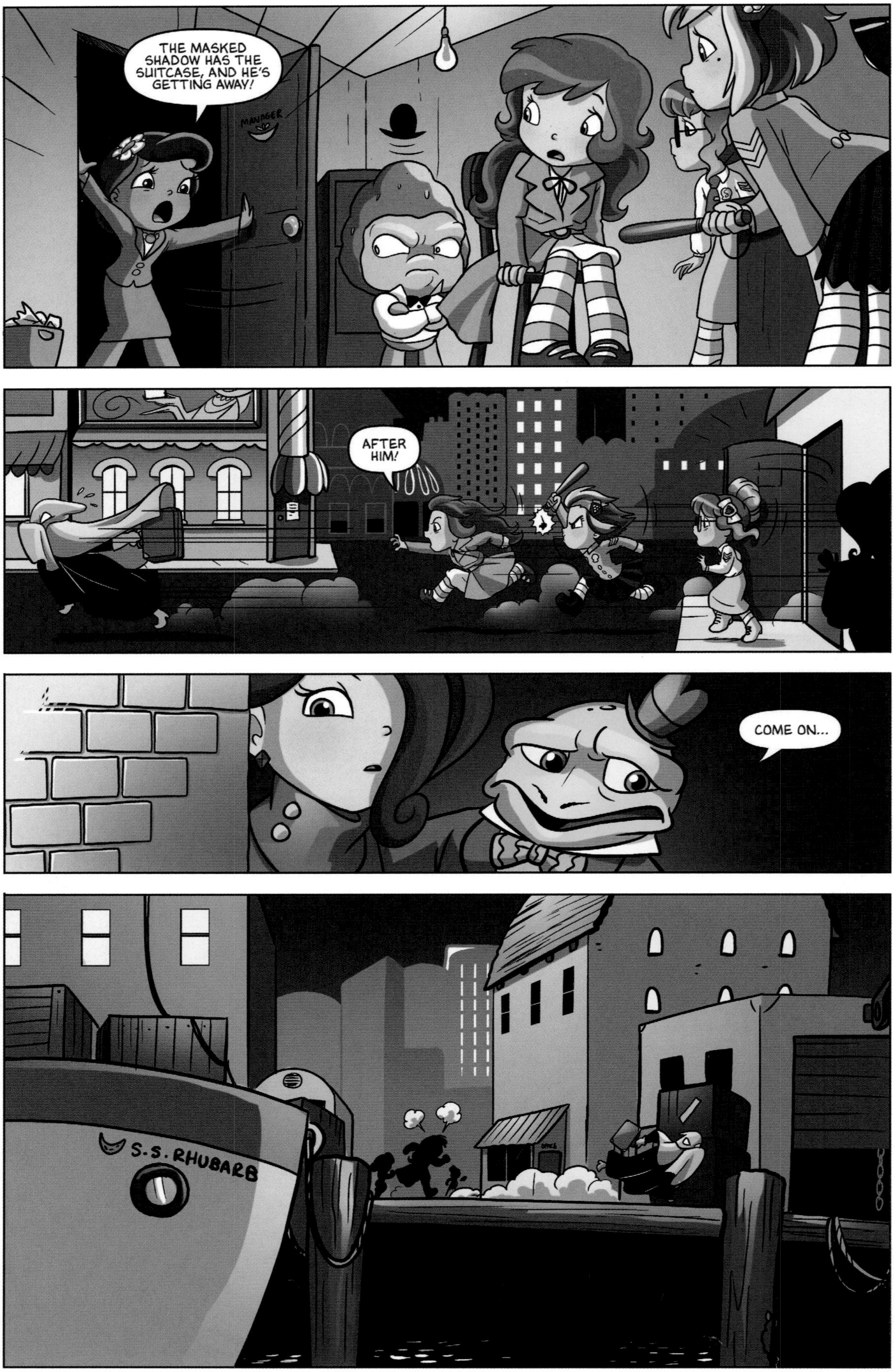
THE MASKED SHADOW HAS THE SUITCASE, AND HE'S GETTING AWAY!
MANAGER
AFTER HIM!
COME ON...
S.S. RHUBARB

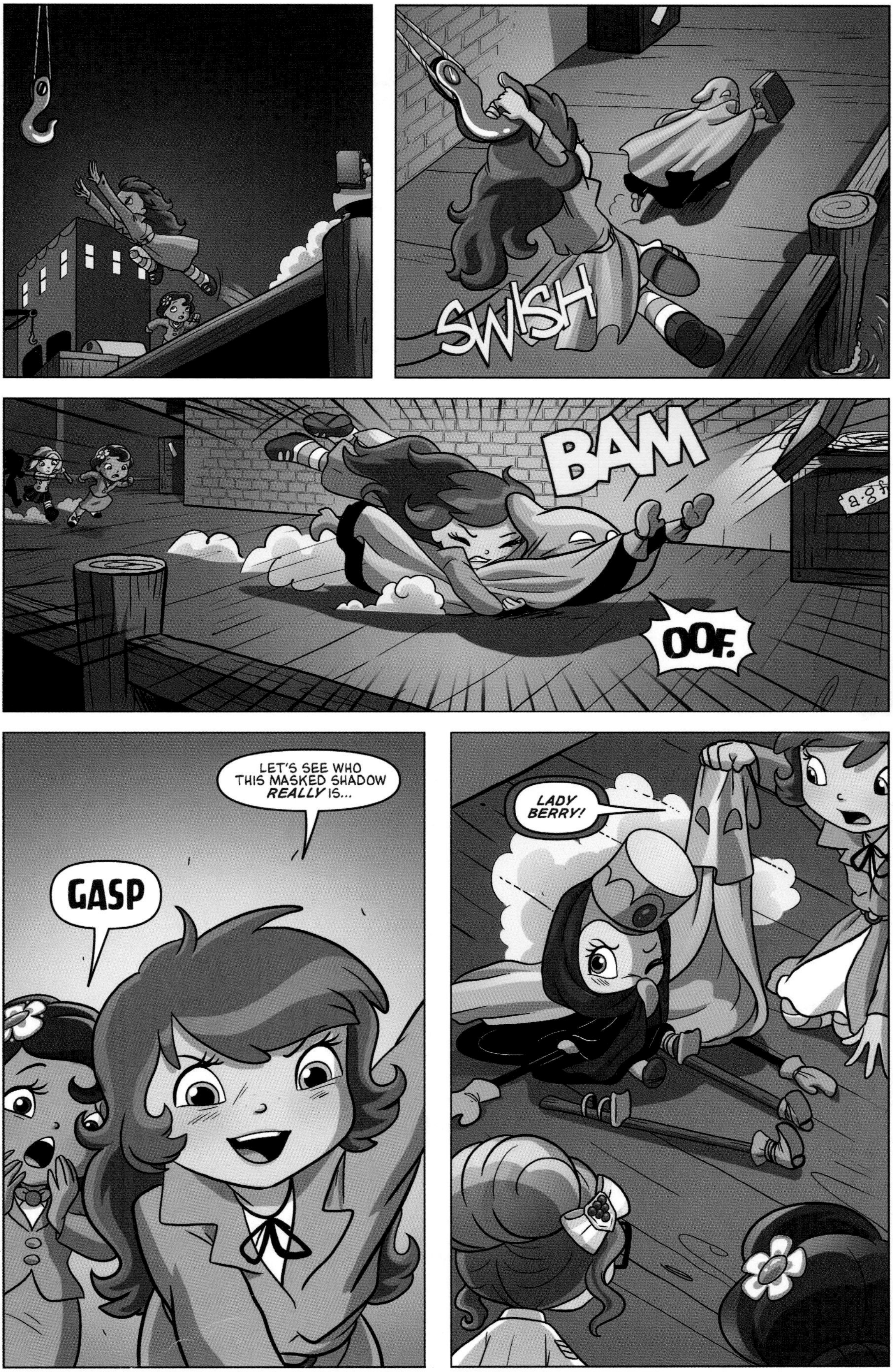
SWISH
BAM
OOF.
LET'S SEE WHO THIS MASKED SHADOW *REALLY* IS...
GASP
LADY BERRY!

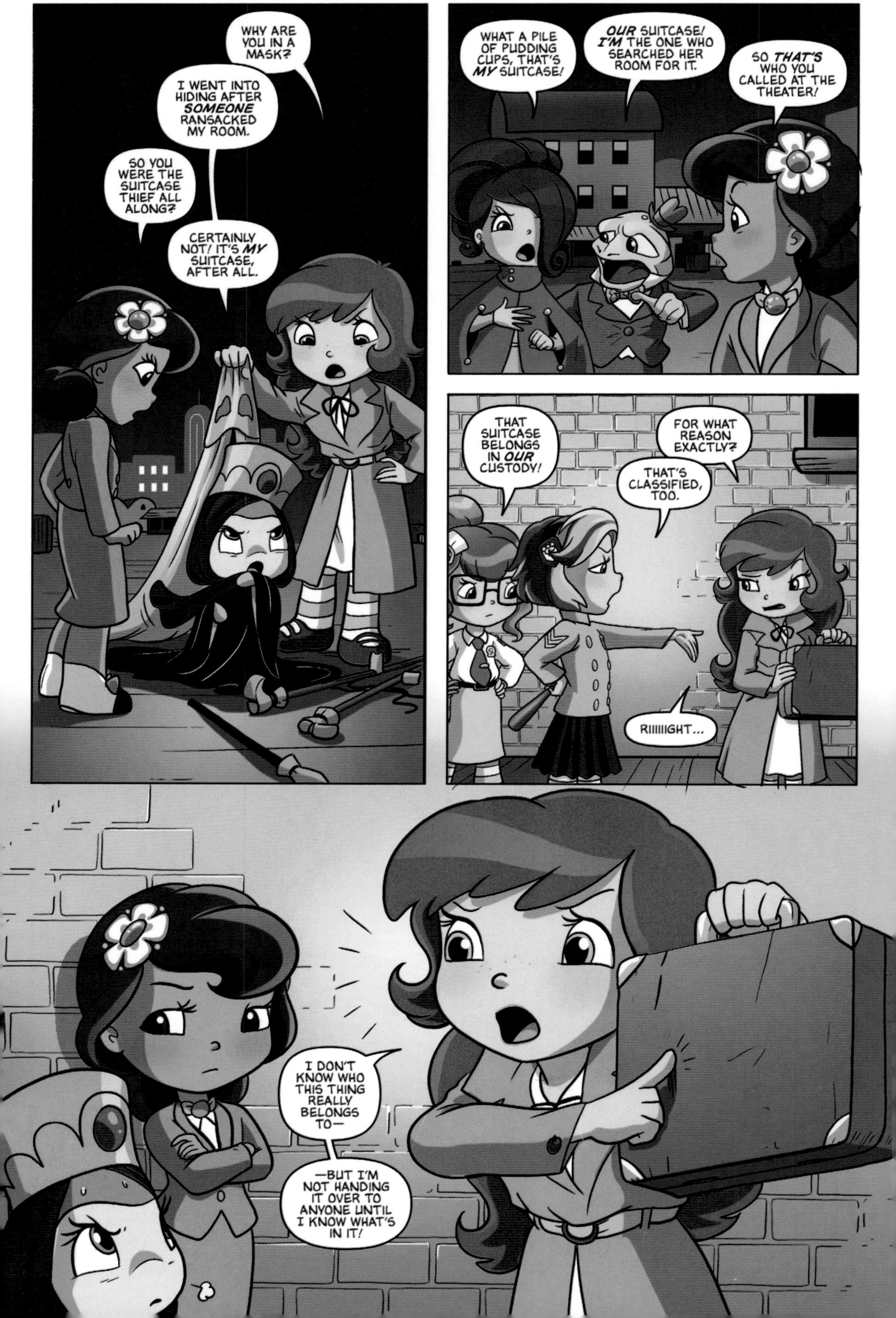
WHY ARE YOU IN A MASK?
I WENT INTO HIDING AFTER SOMEONE RANSACKED MY ROOM.
SO YOU WERE THE SUITCASE THIEF ALL ALONG?
CERTAINLY NOT! IT'S MY SUITCASE, AFTER ALL.
WHAT A PILE OF PUDDING CUPS, THAT'S MY SUITCASE!
OUR SUITCASE! I'M THE ONE WHO SEARCHED HER ROOM FOR IT.
SO THAT'S WHO YOU CALLED AT THE THEATER!
THAT SUITCASE BELONGS IN OUR CUSTODY!
FOR WHAT REASON EXACTLY?
THAT'S CLASSIFIED, TOO.
RIIIIIGHT...
I DON'T KNOW WHO THIS THING REALLY BELONGS TO—
—BUT I'M NOT HANDING IT OVER TO ANYONE UNTIL I KNOW WHAT'S IN IT!

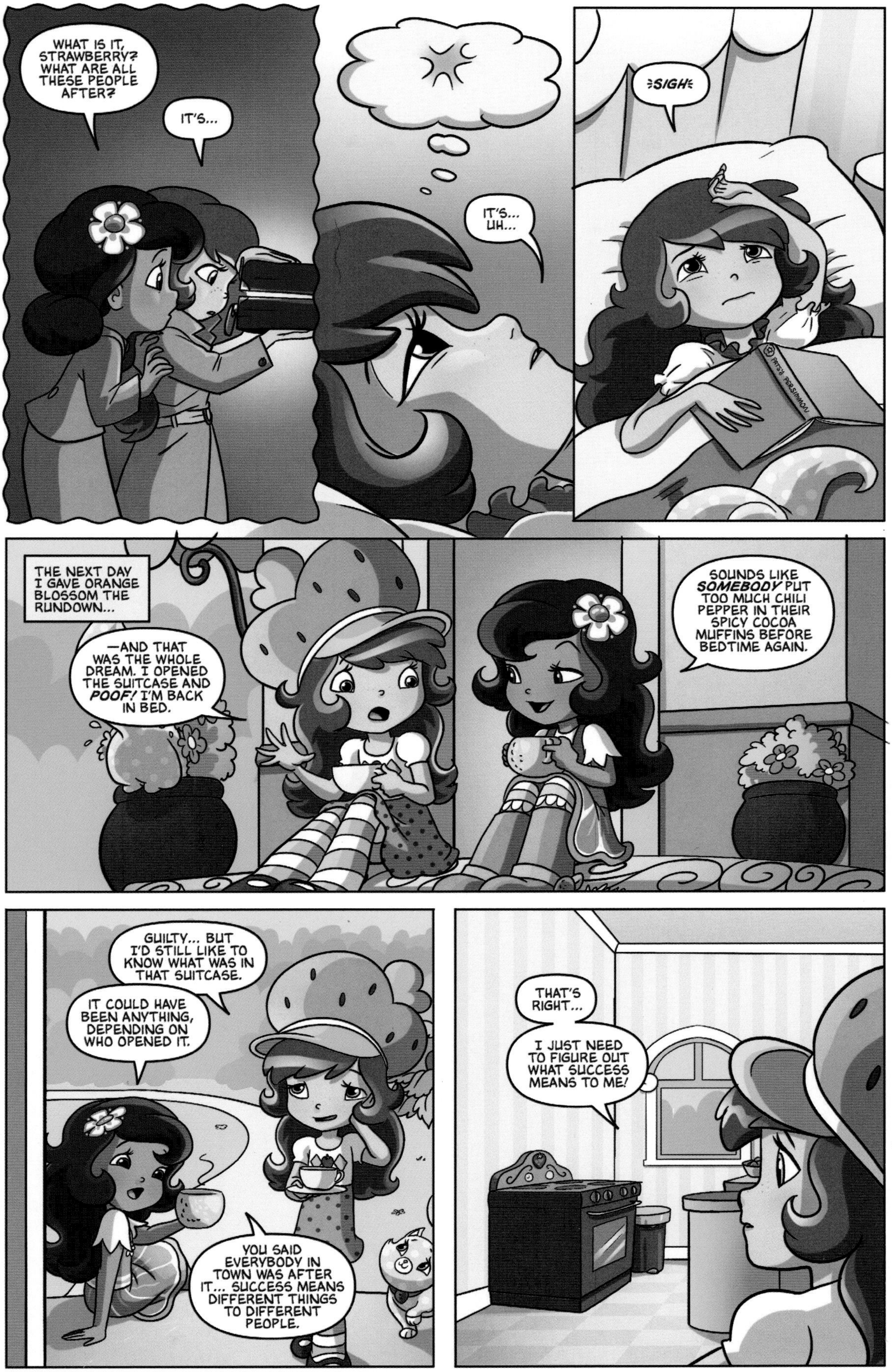
WHAT IS IT, STRAWBERRY? WHAT ARE ALL THESE PEOPLE AFTER?
IT'S...
IT'S... UH...
SIGH
PERSIMMON
THE NEXT DAY I GAVE ORANGE BLOSSOM THE RUNDOWN...
—AND THAT WAS THE WHOLE DREAM. I OPENED THE SUITCASE AND POOF! I'M BACK IN BED.
SOUNDS LIKE SOMEBODY PUT TOO MUCH CHILI PEPPER IN THEIR SPICY COCOA MUFFINS BEFORE BEDTIME AGAIN.
GUILTY... BUT I'D STILL LIKE TO KNOW WHAT WAS IN THAT SUITCASE.
IT COULD HAVE BEEN ANYTHING, DEPENDING ON WHO OPENED IT.
YOU SAID EVERYBODY IN TOWN WAS AFTER IT... SUCCESS MEANS DIFFERENT THINGS TO DIFFERENT PEOPLE.
THAT'S RIGHT...
I JUST NEED TO FIGURE OUT WHAT SUCCESS MEANS TO ME!

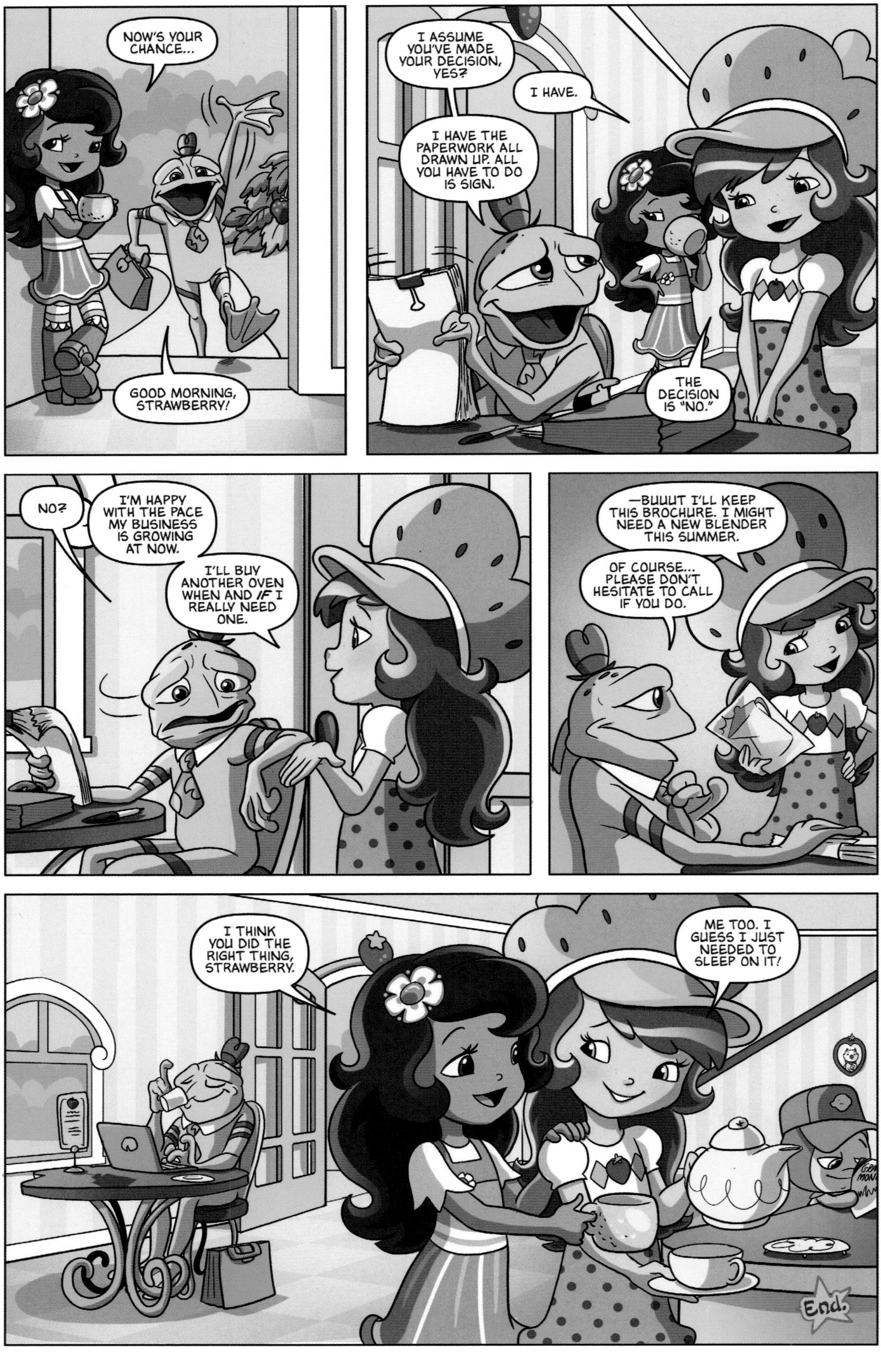
NOW'S YOUR CHANCE...
GOOD MORNING, STRAWBERRY!
I ASSUME YOU'VE MADE YOUR DECISION, YES?
I HAVE.
I HAVE THE PAPERWORK ALL DRAWN UP. ALL YOU HAVE TO DO IS SIGN.
THE DECISION IS "NO."
NO?
I'M HAPPY WITH THE PACE MY BUSINESS IS GROWING AT NOW.
I'LL BUY ANOTHER OVEN WHEN AND IF I REALLY NEED ONE.
—BUUUT I'LL KEEP THIS BROCHURE. I MIGHT NEED A NEW BLENDER THIS SUMMER.
OF COURSE... PLEASE DON'T HESITATE TO CALL IF YOU DO.
I THINK YOU DID THE RIGHT THING, STRAWBERRY.
ME TOO. I GUESS I JUST NEEDED TO SLEEP ON IT!
End.

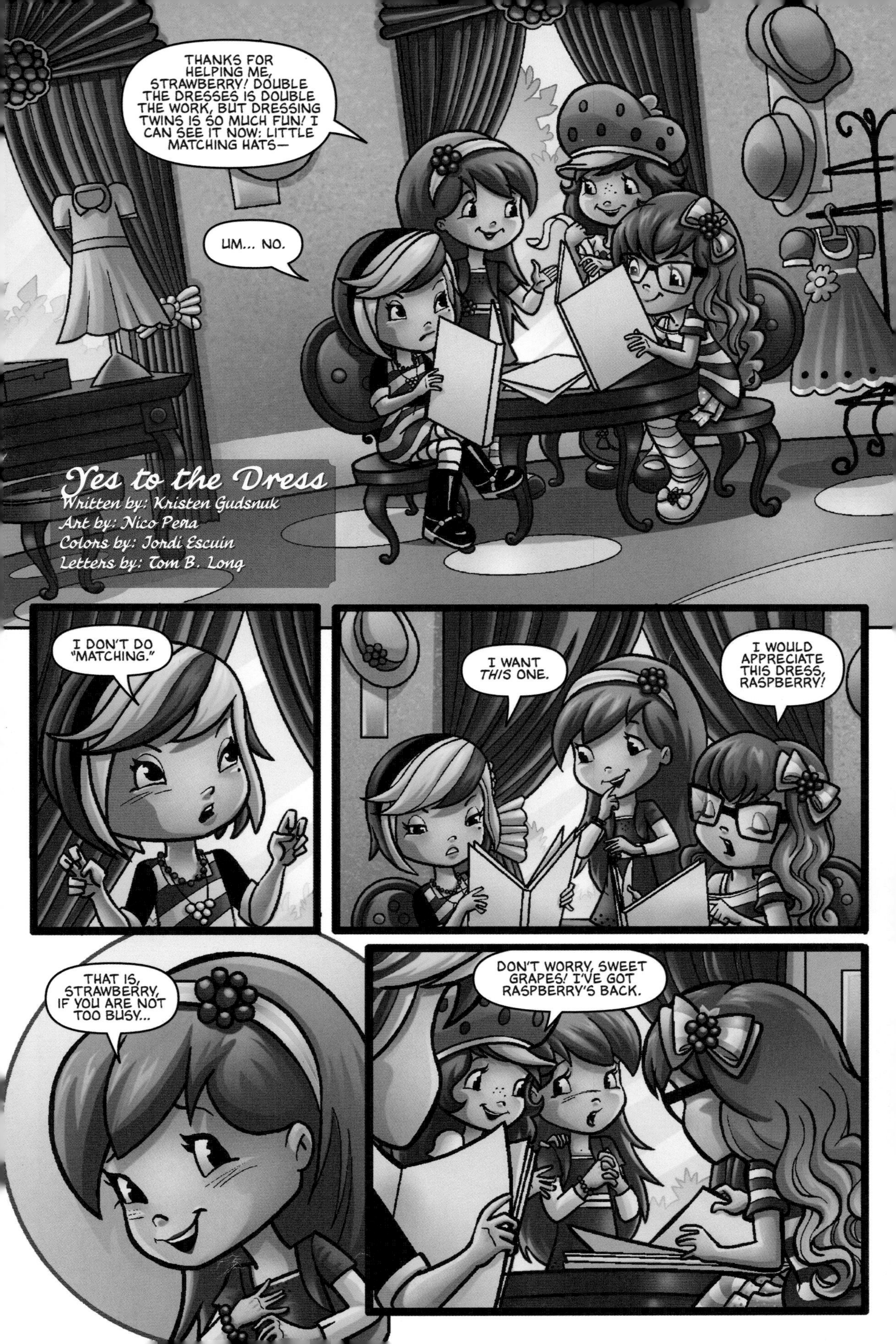
THANKS FOR HELPING ME, STRAWBERRY! DOUBLE THE DRESSES IS DOUBLE THE WORK, BUT DRESSING TWINS IS SO MUCH FUN! I CAN SEE IT NOW: LITTLE MATCHING HATS—
UM... NO.
Yes to the Dress
Written by: Kristen Gudsnuk
Art by: Nico Peña
Colors by: Jordi Escuin
Letters by: Tom B. Long
I DON'T DO "MATCHING."
I WANT THIS ONE.
I WOULD APPRECIATE THIS DRESS, RASPBERRY!
THAT IS, STRAWBERRY, IF YOU ARE NOT TOO BUSY...
DON'T WORRY, SWEET GRAPES! I'VE GOT RASPBERRY'S BACK.

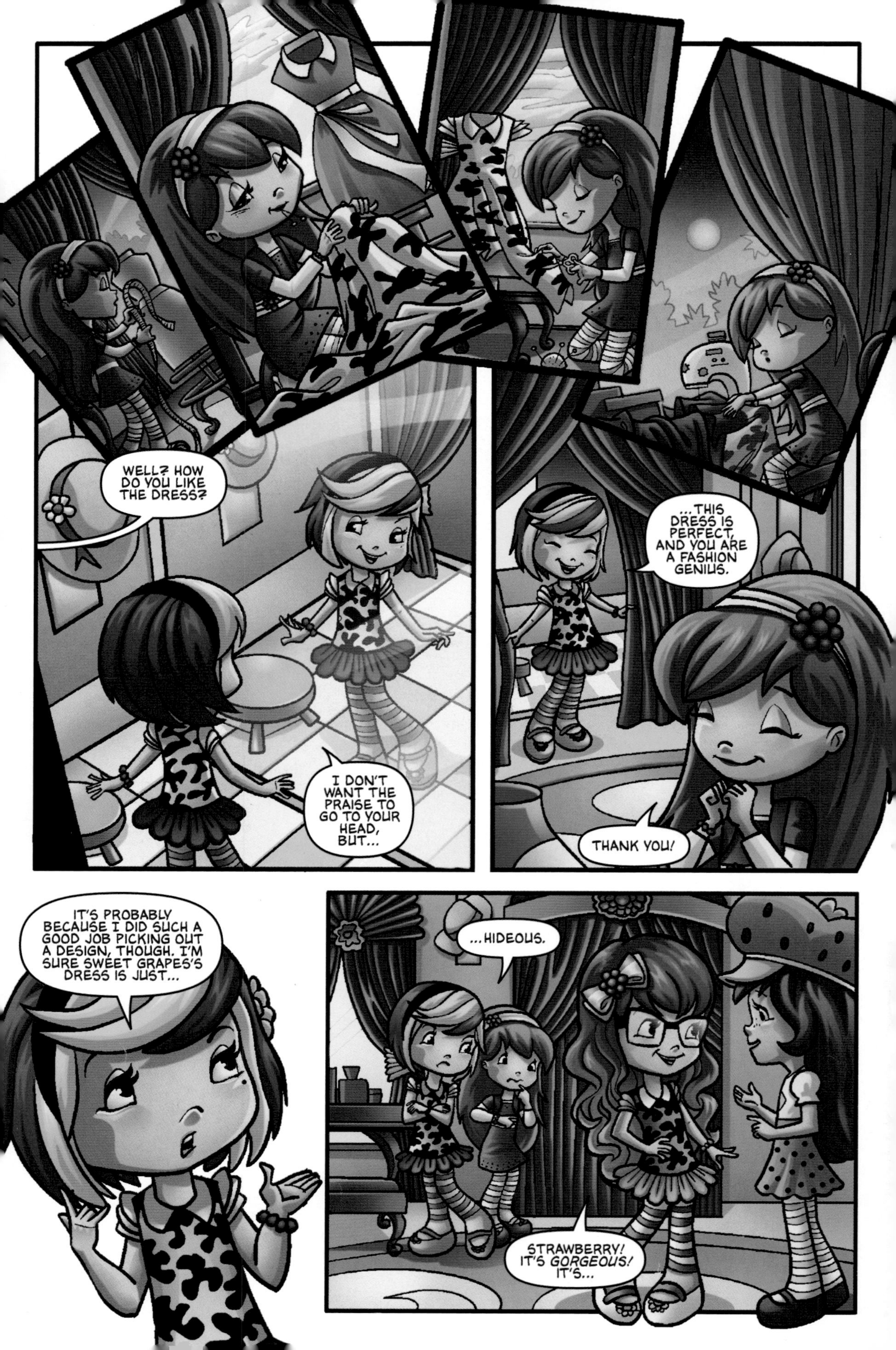
WELL? HOW DO YOU LIKE THE DRESS?
I DON'T WANT THE PRAISE TO GO TO YOUR HEAD, BUT...
...THIS DRESS IS PERFECT, AND YOU ARE A FASHION GENIUS.
THANK YOU!
IT'S PROBABLY BECAUSE I DID SUCH A GOOD JOB PICKING OUT A DESIGN, THOUGH. I'M SURE SWEET GRAPES'S DRESS IS JUST...
...HIDEOUS.
STRAWBERRY! IT'S *GORGEOUS!* IT'S...

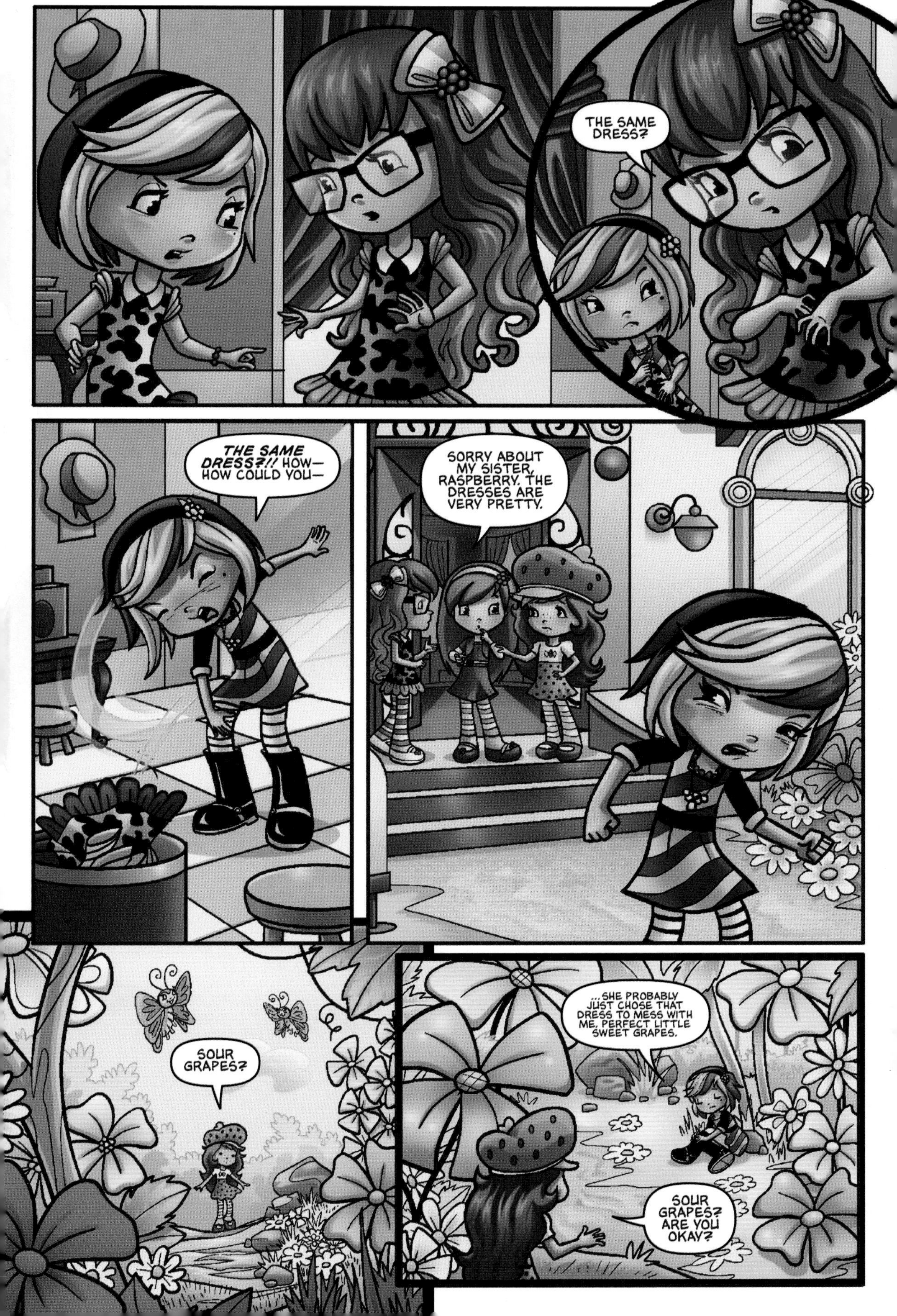
THE SAME DRESS?
THE SAME DRESS?!! HOW—HOW COULD YOU—
SORRY ABOUT MY SISTER, RASPBERRY. THE DRESSES ARE VERY PRETTY.
SOUR GRAPES?
...SHE PROBABLY JUST CHOSE THAT DRESS TO MESS WITH ME. PERFECT LITTLE SWEET GRAPES.
SOUR GRAPES? ARE YOU OKAY?

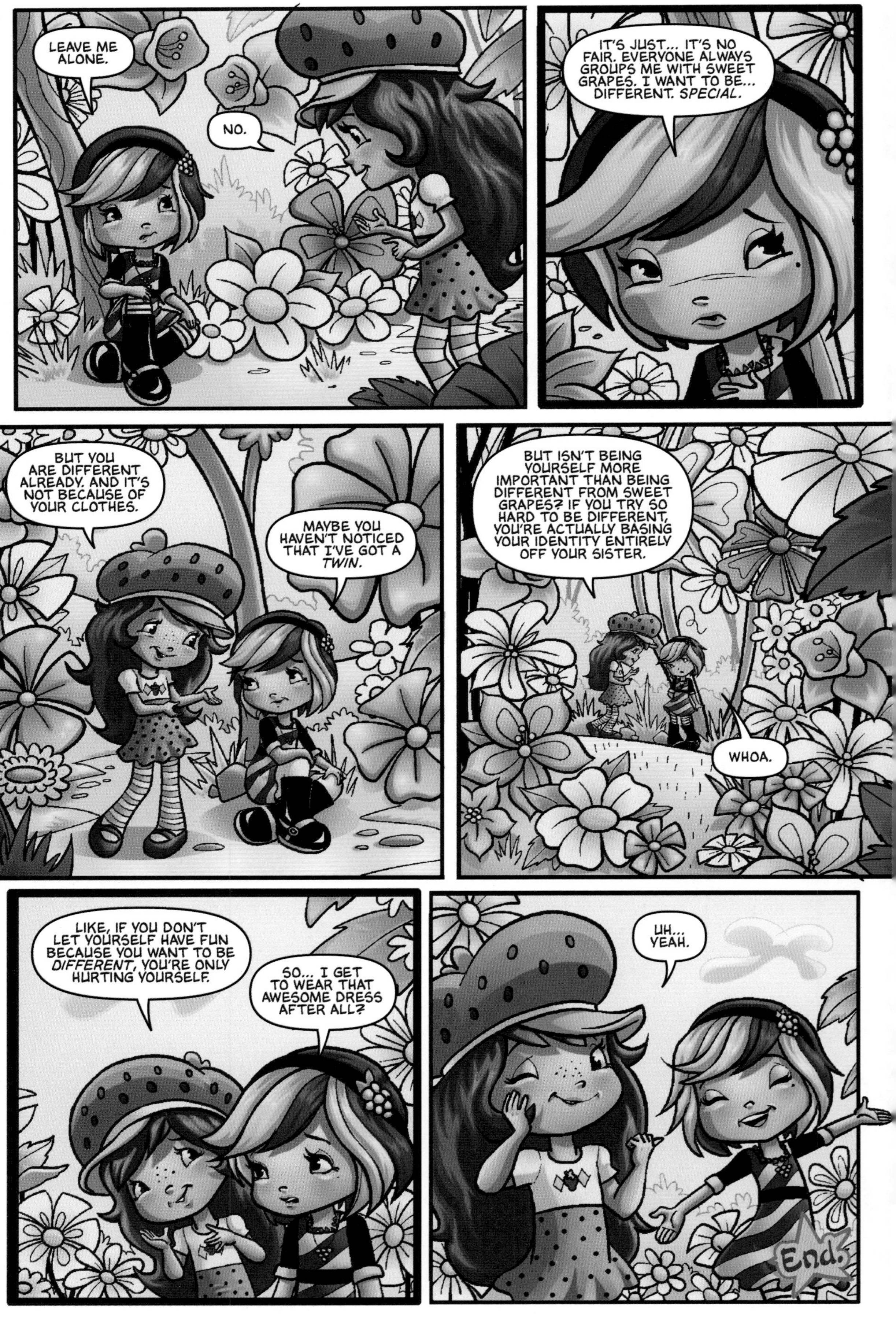
LEAVE ME ALONE.
NO.
IT'S JUST... IT'S NO FAIR. EVERYONE ALWAYS GROUPS ME WITH SWEET GRAPES. I WANT TO BE... DIFFERENT. *SPECIAL.*
BUT YOU ARE DIFFERENT ALREADY. AND IT'S NOT BECAUSE OF YOUR CLOTHES.
MAYBE YOU HAVEN'T NOTICED THAT I'VE GOT A *TWIN.*
BUT ISN'T BEING YOURSELF MORE IMPORTANT THAN BEING DIFFERENT FROM SWEET GRAPES? IF YOU TRY SO HARD TO BE DIFFERENT, YOU'RE ACTUALLY BASING YOUR IDENTITY ENTIRELY OFF YOUR SISTER.
WHOA.
LIKE, IF YOU DON'T LET YOURSELF HAVE FUN BECAUSE YOU WANT TO BE *DIFFERENT*, YOU'RE ONLY HURTING YOURSELF.
SO... I GET TO WEAR THAT AWESOME DRESS AFTER ALL?
UH... YEAH.
End.

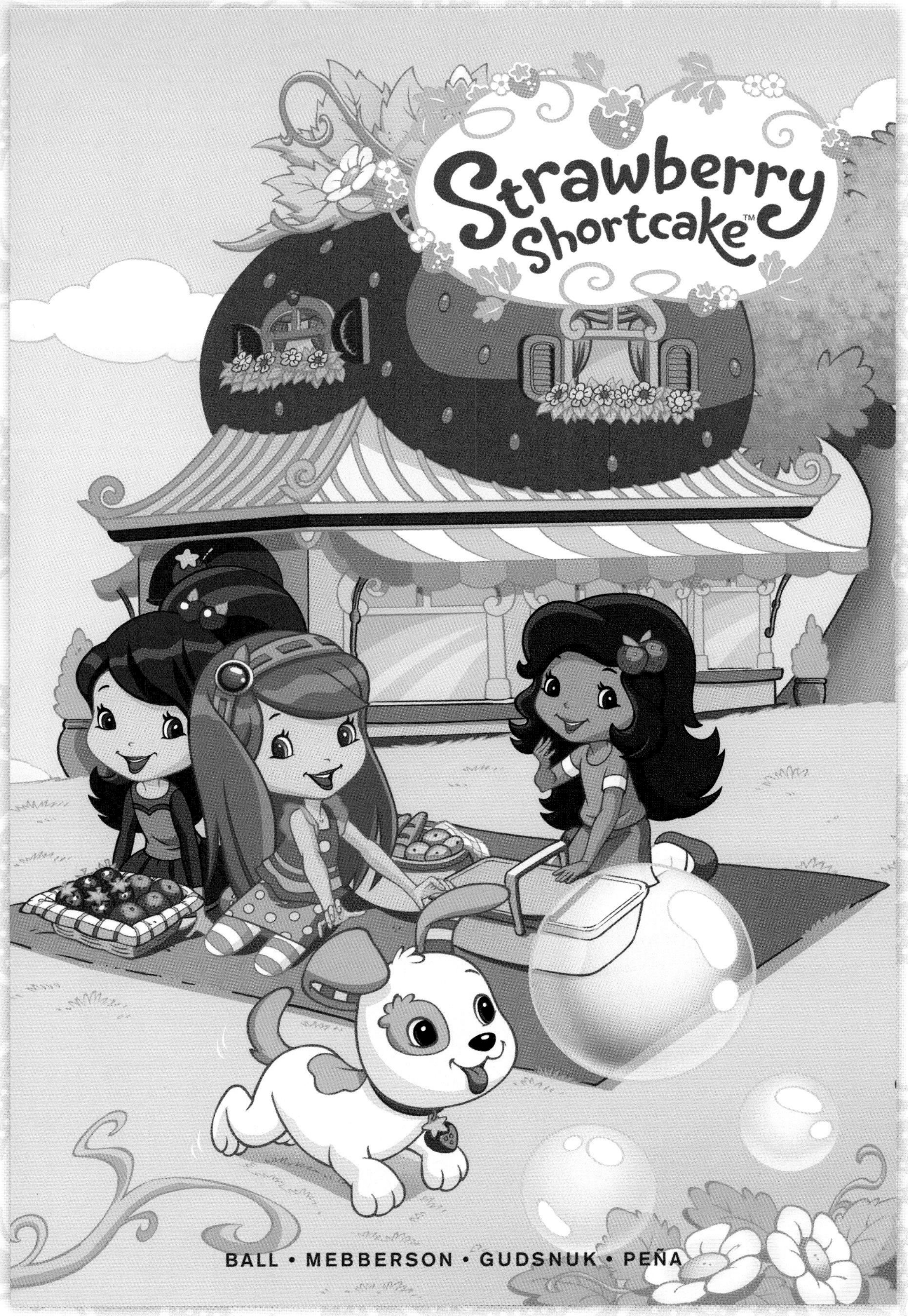
Strawberry Shortcake™
BALL • MEBBERSON • GUDSNUK • PEÑA

STRAWBERRY SHORTCAKE ISSUE #3, SUB COVER
art by Tina Francisco and colors by Mae Hao

Strawberry Shortcake™

COLLECT THEM ALL!

Set of 6 Hardcover Books ISBN: 978-1-5321-4028-0

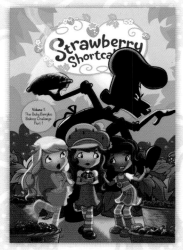

Strawberry Shortcake

Hardcover Book ISBN 978-1-5321-4029-7

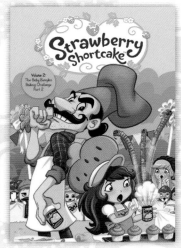

Strawberry Shortcake

Hardcover Book ISBN 978-1-5321-4030-3

Strawberry Shortcake

Hardcover Book ISBN 978-1-5321-4031-0

Strawberry Shortcake

Hardcover Book ISBN 978-1-5321-4032-7

Strawberry Shortcake

Hardcover Book ISBN 978-1-5321-4033-4

Strawberry Shortcake

Hardcover Book ISBN 978-1-5321-4034-1